Sonny's Dream

Noriko Senshu

HR

for the evolving human spirit

HAMPTON ROADS
PUBLISHING COMPANY, INC.

Hampton Roads Publishing Company is dedicated to providing quality children's books that stimulate the intellect, teach valuable lessons, and allow our children's spirits to grow. We have created our line of Young Spirit Books for the evolving human spirit of our children. Give your children Young Spirit Books—their key to a whole new world!

Hampton Roads Publishing Company publishes books on a variety of subjects including metaphysics, health, complementary medicine, visionary fiction, and other related topics.

For a copy of our latest catalog, call toll-free, 800-766-8009,
or send your name and address to:

Hampton Roads Publishing Company, Inc.
1125 Stoney Ridge Road
Charlottesville, VA 22902
email: hrpc@hrpub.com
www.hrpub.com

Cover design by Grace Pedalino

For information write:

Hampton Roads Publishing Company, Inc.
1125 Stoney Ridge Road
Charlottesville, VA 22902

Or call: 804-296-2772
FAX: 804-296-5096
e-mail: hrpc@hrpub.com
Web site: www.hrpub.com

If you are unable to order this book from your local
bookseller, you may order directly from the publisher.
Call 1-800-766-8009, toll-free.

Library of Congress Catalog Card Number: 00-10920
ISBN 1-57174-215-8
10 9 8 7 6 5 4 3 2 1
Printed on acid-free paper in China

To all friends who have bad dreams . . .

I can remember . . .

Inside the dark and cozy den,
I was covered all over by Mother's nice, warm fur—a soft futon.
It rocked along with her long, deep breath and
crooned a sweet lullaby to the rhythm of her heart.

The floating music carried me out of the den
   back to my first summer.

   Dazzling light stretched down from above,
      and swirling bubbles rose from my mouth.

   The bubbling sound echoed,
      and it echoed down to the river where I dropped—PLOP!

A strong current surged over me.
It stung my belly.
I saw them come towards me,
a school of Red Monster Fish.

I was scared. Those Monster Fish showed up right before my nose.
Struck dumb with horror, my ears popped, my mouth dried,
my belly rumbled, my hind legs cramped.

Goggle-eyed Monster Fish stared at me.
Reflected light on their sharp glaring teeth made me dazed and dizzy.

Grrr, Aaaahhh!!

Just in the nick of time, something much bigger and more fierce
sucked up all the Monster Fish.

Grrr, Aaaahhh!!

I snuggled up to my fluffy futon.

Grrr, Aaaahhh!!

My futon shook me off.

I awoke to find myself in the den, nestling close to Mother.
Spring sun softly poured in.
A touch of light tickled my furry ears.

Out of the den, I took a big sniff.
My belly was empty and I felt groggy.
"Sonny, it's time to learn how to get your own food.
Follow what I do, and learn from me," said Mother.
So I did.

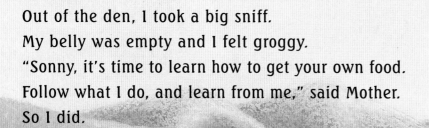

Mother sniffed along the ground, and I sniffed along the ground.
Mother dashed off to catch a ground squirrel.
I dashed off to catch up with her.
I watched Mother eat a squirrel and waited for a share.

After practicing all spring,
I caught my first squirrel.

Grrr, Aaaahhh!!

I ate the whole thing.

After enough of the ground squirrels, Mother took me to the river.
Big silvery fish jumped against the current.
My bad dream splashed over me.
I told Mother about the Red Monster Fish.

"Oh, my poor little baby!" she said.
"Listen. Salmon like this travel upstream, and change to red
towards the end of their journey.
Last summer, when you were a teeny-weeny cub,
you fell in midstream among the big fat red salmon.
It must have scared you.
But Sonny, now you are big enough to catch salmon.
You just need some practice."

Mother scooped up a fresh plump salmon.
She tossed me the fish's tail,
and it tasted a lot better than the squirrels.
I wanted to eat the whole thing.
So I practiced, swish-swash, swish-swash . . . all summer long.

By the next summer, catching food became easy.
I ate lots of ground squirrels and fish.
I grew into a strong and stout Grizzly.
Following Mother's lead, I had nothing to be afraid of.

I was a little surprised when Mother said,

"Sonny, now, to be an adult Grizzly, you have one big lesson to learn.
Without my help, you will make a decision on your own.
Without my help, you will make a choice of your own.
It will come soon."

That felt fine with me.
I knew, with practice, I could overcome anything.
Mother and I walked around the willow bush through the tundra.
On a gentle breeze, a butterfly flew into my sight.
Amused by the dancing butterfly, I forgot what Mother said to me.

I ran to-and-fro after the flittering butterfly.
I nibbled here and there at the lowbush cranberries.
I wandered far and away, far from Mother.

I looked back for Mother.
She was out of sight.
I rested near the willows and waited for her to come for me.
My body felt stiff and strange with worry and fear.

My heart beat with the Land of the Midnight Sun.
Mother's words flashed across my mind.
Was this the lesson she'd meant? Aauuhhh . . .

I felt so hungry.
I set off to catch food.
That was my own choice.
If I practiced this, Mother would be back.

The world changed as the leaves turned red and yellow.
A wind from the Arctic blew the leaves off the trees.
The rising north wind howled, and I roared for Mother.

When an early snow fell,
I roamed the valley seeking a den.
I found a cozy spot and settled down for a long winter sleep.

Covered with deep snow, the land was still.
Across the endless night sky,
the Northern Lights spread their ever-changing colors.
Their reflection melted into a shine over my den.
Under a blanket of Northern Lights, I slept soundly.

The flow of lights gracefully changed its shape,
in and out, on and off, in the dark sky.
It played a mystical tune in harmony.
All over the frigid land, the music of lights whispered.
Drawn to the melody, a school of Red Monster Fish came over toward me.
I shivered with fear.

Monster Fish gazed at me with teeth bared.
They liked the sight of my dread.
Not knowing what to do, I breathed hard.
I felt all alone.

So I roared and roared from deep in my belly.

GRRR, AAAAHHH!!
"GO AWAY! THIS IS MY PROPERTY!!"

Those Red Monster Fish turned and faded into the distance.
Feeling brave and strong, I marched out of my dream.

The birth of spring showed everywhere.
I sniffed along.
A ground squirrel crept out of its hole.
I caught it in one bound, and ate it in one bite.
One after another, I caught more squirrels and enjoyed a good feast.

As I strolled about,
snow melted away in the tundra, and the bushes came into bud.
I came to a small valley filled with leafy trees.
Spring breezes stirred the leaves.
I melted into an endless mountain range spread out to the far horizon.

Bathed in the long daylight,
the leaves laid a green carpet over the land.
The river rumbled as salmon migrated up the stream.
Splash-splosh, splosh-splash,
I aimed at the approaching fish one by one, and made good catches.
Stuffed with juicy fish, I cast the tails away.

I strolled in my territory.

Headed to my favorite hill, I gulped the ripe berries.

On top of the hill, I looked over my world.

In the distance, I spotted a Grizzly mother and her two cubs.

Clumsy little cubs clambered on their mother

only to tumble off and roll over.

Poor little ones, they had lots of lessons to learn.

Leaves rustled in the wind.
Bits of dandelion fluff blew past my nose and drifted into the sky.
Soaked in the glow of the midnight sun,
I listened to the music:
The birds' chirps and tweets in soprano.
The steady flow of running water in bass.
Cradled in peaceful harmony, I dozed off.

I dreamed . . .
I conquered the Monster Fish.
With the prize in my mouth, I swam across the stream.

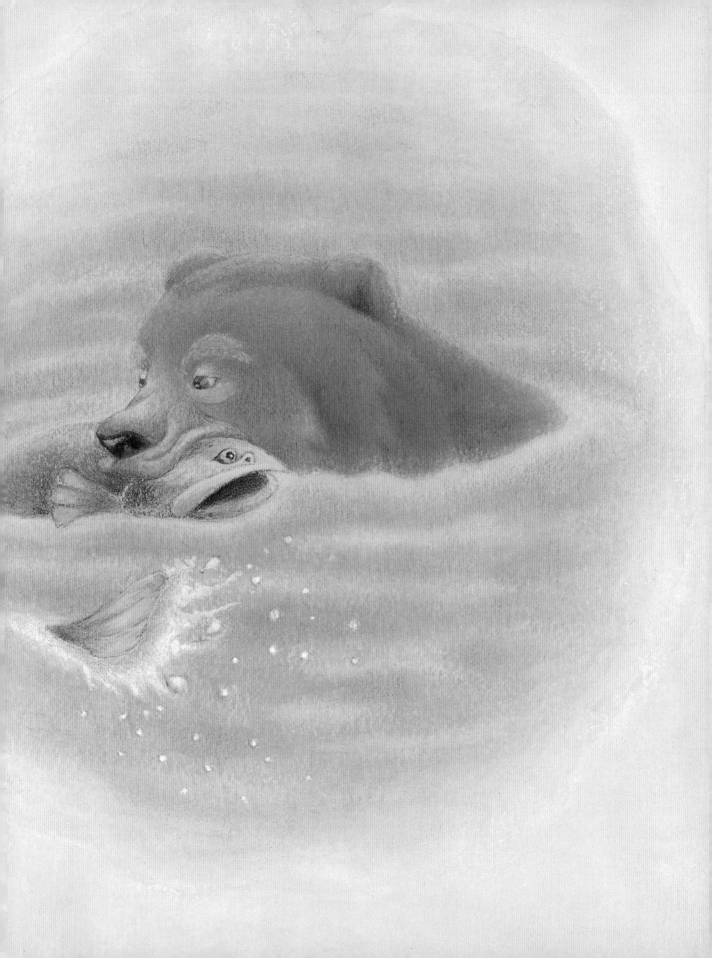

And that's how I became a master fisher
in the Land of the Midnight Sun,
through long winter sleep
in my dreams
in the Land of the Northern Lights.